W9-CHI-123

For Flory

Copyright © 1988 by Kady MacDonald Denton
First published by Walker Books, Ltd., London
All rights reserved. No part of this book may be reproduced or transmitted
in any form or by any means, electronic or mechanical, including photocopying,
recording, or by any information storage and retrieval system,
without permission in writing from the Publisher.

Margaret K. McElderry Books
Macmillan Publishing Company
866 Third Avenue
New York, NY 10022
Collier Macmillan Canada, Inc.

First United States Edition 1988

Printed in Italy

10 9 8 7 6 5 4 3 2 1

Library of Congress Cataloging-in-Publication Data

Denton, Kady MacDonald.
Granny is a darling.

Summary: When Billy shares his room with Granny one
night, he learns something to banish his bedtime fears
ever after.
[1. Bedtime—Fiction.   2. Grandmothers—Fiction]
I. Title.
PZ7.D436Gr 1988   [E]   87-22635
ISBN 0-689-50452-7

GRANNY

IS A
DARLING

Kady MacDonald Denton

Margaret K. McElderry Books
NEW YORK

ATHENS REGIONAL LIBRARY
ATHENS, GEORGIA

403511

"Granny is a darling," said everyone in Billy's family. "It's so nice when she comes to visit."

Billy thought so too. He ran to hug her.
She was his *granny*!

Granny had a little something for everyone.

Billy thought his picture was best of all.
"We'll hang it near your bed," said Granny.
"I hope you don't mind sharing your room
with me tonight."

Billy didn't mind at all. He would sleep
in his old cot.

Later, Billy watched his granny getting
ready for bed. Should he tell her that
scary things sometimes came
into his room at night?

"Are you afraid of the dark,
Granny?" he asked.

"Oh, I go straight to sleep," she said.
"Now you go straight to sleep, too."

Billy pulled up his
covers. The room was
quiet and very dark.

Something at
the window was
very
VERY
dark.

By the door,
what was that?

In the wardrobe,
what was that!

Strange noises filled the room.

Sssnnnorrrrr! sssssZZZZZ!

Billy jumped out of bed. The scary
things must not hurt his granny.

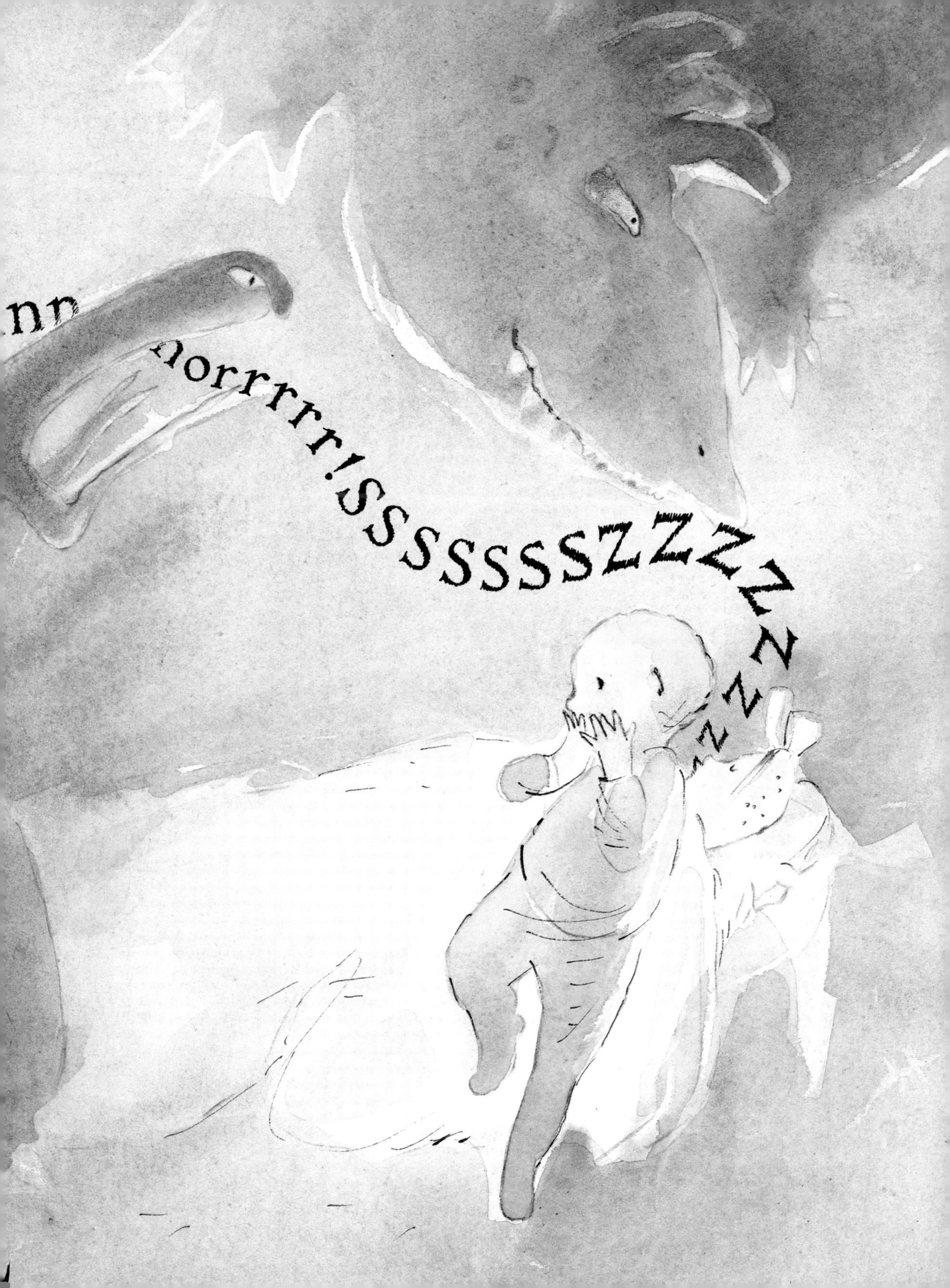
nn
norrrrr!SSSSSSZZZZZZZZ

Billy saw that his granny was
asleep. Her mouth was wide open.

SSSSSSSSSSSSNNNNOR

The dark things backed away.

POP! went the dark things by the door.
"SSSSNNNORRRR! SSSSSSSZZZZZZ!"
went Billy, as loud as he could – just like
his granny.

Billy pulled up his granny's covers.
"It's all right, Granny," he said,
"they're gone now."

He hopped back into bed, feeling suddenly very sleepy.

When Billy woke, his granny was already up and dressed.

"I hope you slept well, Billy," she said. "I snore sometimes, you know."

Billy smiled. "Yes," he said, "I know."

Granny *was* a darling.

That night, after Granny had gone,
Billy was all alone in his room.

It was quiet and very dark.

Billy looked at the picture on his wall.

"SSSSNNNORRRR!" he went, just
like his granny.

Then he closed
his eyes and fell
fast asleep.

T9236

403511

E   Denton, Kady
DEN   MacDonald.

      Granny is a darling

$12.95

DATE			

ATHENS REGIONAL LIBRARY
ATHENS, GEORGIA

© THE BAKER & TAYLOR CO.